Pete and Johnny to the Rescue

by Jørgen Clevin

RANDOM HOUSE NEW YORK

First American Edition 1974

Copyright © 1974 by Random House, Inc. All rights reserved under International and Pan-American Copyright Conventions. Published in the United States by Random House, Inc., New York. Originally published in Denmark as *Jacob og Joakims Redningskorps* by Gyldendalske Boghandel, Copenhagen. Copyright © 1971 by Jørgen Clevin.

Manufactured in the United States of America   1 2 3 4 5 6 7 8 9 0

NOTE: *You will see that there are questions*
for you to answer when you read this book.
Every time you come to a red light
please stop and answer the question.

Pete and Johnny live at number 14 Flower Street.
Johnny is a little boy and Pete is an elephant.
While Johnny takes care of the house and cooks the food,
Pete goes to school.

Right now they are in the backyard,
working in their garden.

Shall we go say hello to them?

"Welcome to our garden," says Johnny.
"What's *your* name?"

"Welcome to our garden," says Pete the elephant.
"I go to school every day, but Friday will be my last day.
After that I'm going to get a job."

Have *you* ever had a job?

Pete likes school.
He shares a desk with his friend Jasper Mouse.
At lunchtime they even share their sandwiches.

Pete has a yellow schoolbag.
What do *you* think he carries in it?

On Friday morning, Pete leaves the house very early.
He is taking a flower to Miss Lottie, his teacher,
because it is the last day of school.

"I'm glad Johnny woke me up so early," Pete says.

Who wakes *you* up in the morning?

Why is Pete taking a flower to Miss Lottie?

All the animals are early today.
They are in the schoolyard at five minutes to eight.
Each one has a flower for Miss Lottie.
   "Here you are, Miss Lottie," they cry.
"Here is a little flower from me to you!"

How many animals go to Miss Lottie's school?

When the animals go into the classroom,
they find a surprise waiting for them.

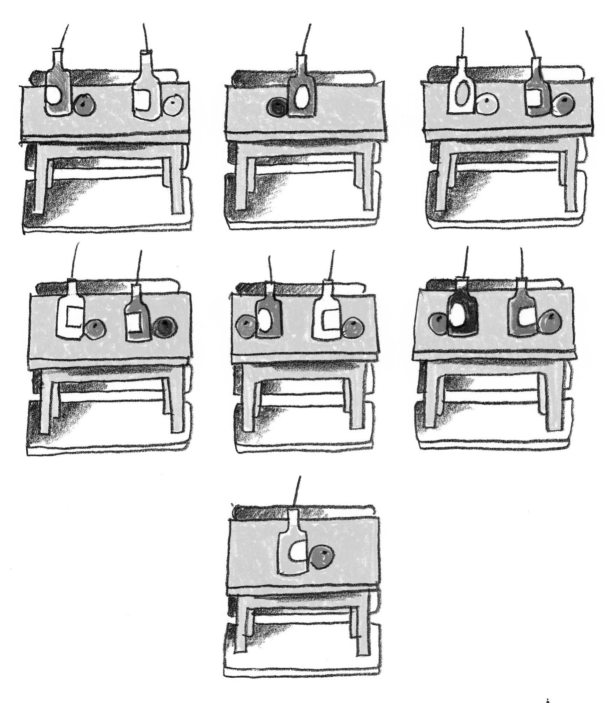

What has Miss Lottie brought for her students?

What kind of soda do *you* like best?

Since it is the last day of school
the animals play games.
They are playing WHO AM I?
You can play, too.

I say *bow wow* and watch the house. Who am I?

I say *meow meow* and drink milk. Who am I?

I say *tweet tweet* and live up in the trees.

I say *cock-a-doodle-doo* and wake people up in the morning.

I say *squeak squeak* and hide in a hole.

I say *dingalingaling* when school is over.

I say *toot toot* and sail on the ocean.

I say *moo moo* and give you fresh milk.

I say *baa baa* and my coat gives you wool for sweaters.

I say *oink oink* and have a curl in my tail.

I say *honk honk* and use gasoline for fuel.

I say *tick tock* and show you what time it is.

I say *tatatat* and make beautiful music.

I say *whoo whoo* and run on tracks.

"Now let's pretend that we go to Miss Lottie's school!" says Jasper Mouse. "And we are having a party with soda and apples."

"That's a good idea!" says Miss Lottie.

For a few minutes everybody is busy drinking soda and eating delicious apples.

"Now it's my turn to choose a game!" cries Owl. "Let's play WHAT AM I?"

"Yes, yes," cry all the animals.

Miss Lottie uses me when it is raining. What am I?

Mr. Johnson the carpenter uses me to cut wood. What am I?

Would *you* like to play this game, too?

Look at the pictures and see if you can make up more questions.

When everyone has had a turn Miss Lottie says: "School is over for the year. It's time to go home."

"Thank you for a wonderful year," says Pete. "And thank you for teaching us so many things."

"Good-by, good-by," they all shout.

That night Pete says to Johnny:
"Now that school is over I must get a job."
"We can talk about that tomorrow," says Johnny.
"Now it's time to go to bed."

What time do *you* go to bed at night?

Johnny tucks Pete into bed and turns off the light.
"Please leave the light on," says Pete.
"Then I can sleep better."

Do *you* like to have the light on when you go to sleep?

Pete falls asleep very quickly.
He dreams about all the jobs he might have.
What jobs do *you* think he is dreaming about?

Look at the pictures and see if they give you
some good ideas.

At three minutes past nine the next morning,
Pete jumps out of bed.

"Good morning," says Johnny. "Did you have
pleasant dreams?"

"Yes," Pete answers. "I dreamt about all kinds of jobs.
I wish I could have a job where I would be helping people."

"We could start a Rescue Squad," says Johnny.
"A Rescue Squad helps people."

"That sounds great," says Pete. "Let's do it."

Did *you* ever hear of a Rescue Squad?

How do *you* think it would help people?

First, Pete and Johnny buy
some lumber and nails.
They use them to build a big red garage.
The garage will be their office.
Then they build a high tower
so people will always know where to find them.
They put a large P and a large J
on top of the tower.

What do *you* think the P and J stand for?

Which is highest: the tower, the office, or the house?

After all that building, Johnny and Pete are very tired.
They fall asleep quickly.

Where is Johnny's uniform?

Where are Pete's
red rubber boots?

Early the next morning, Pete and Johnny
are waiting for calls.

Dingalingaling. The telephone is ringing already.
"Hello, hello," says Johnny. "This is Pete and Johnny's
Rescue Squad. We help everyone—big and small.
Just tell me calmly what has happened.
And we will come right over to help you."

"Hello, this is Mike the bus driver. My bus has fallen apart
in the middle of Main Street. One of the back wheels came off
and one of the front wheels has a puncture. The door won't
close, the steering wheel is broken, and the brakes don't work.
What's more, the windshield is cracked and the horn won't
stop honking."
"Oh, we can fix all that," says Johnny. "We'll be right there."

Do *you* think Pete and Johnny
will be able to fix the bus?

Pete and Johnny rush to the rescue!
They can't fix the bus,
but they can take the passengers
where they want to go.

Do *you* ever ride on the bus?

Where do *you* like to sit?

Pete carries the passengers all over town.
After his last trip he is very tired.
   "That was hard work," says Pete.
"I wonder what will happen next."

How do Pete and Johnny help the bus driver?

At nine o'clock the telephone rings again: *Dingalingaling*!

"Hello, hello," says Johnny. "This is Pete and Johnny's
Rescue Squad. We help everyone both big and small.
Just tell me calmly what has happened.
And we will come right over to help you."

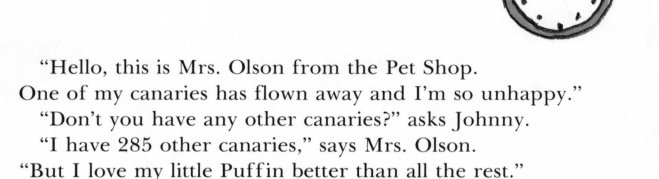

"Hello, this is Mrs. Olson from the Pet Shop.
One of my canaries has flown away and I'm so unhappy."

"Don't you have any other canaries?" asks Johnny.

"I have 285 other canaries," says Mrs. Olson.
"But I love my little Puffin better than all the rest."

"Don't worry," says Johnny. "We will find your little Puffin."

Where is the canary sitting?

Pete and Johnny are lucky. Puffin flies right into the cage and Johnny shuts the door. Mrs. Olson is very happy.

How does Johnny get up high enough
to rescue Mrs. Olson's canary?

At ten o'clock, the doorbell rings.

"I see a lot of children outside," says Pete.

Johnny opens the door.

"This is Pete and Johnny's Rescue Squad," he says.

"We help everyone both big and small.

What can we do for you?"

"There is no one at the playground," the children explain.

"Will you come and play with us?"

"We'll be right over," says Johnny.

What are the names of *your* best friends?

Do *you* like to play at the playground?

Pete and Johnny hurry to the playground.
The children have a wonderful time with them.
What do *you* play when you go to the playground?

"It's not easy to play with small children," says Pete.
"Do you think we could go home soon? I need to rest."

But Pete does not have time to rest.
As soon as he gets home the telephone rings again.
    "Hello, hello," says Johnny. "This is Pete and
Johnny's Rescue Squad. We help everyone
both big and small."

    "Hello, this is Jerry. I'm camping in the woods.
I started a fire with matches, but I don't know how
to put it out. I'm afraid the trees will catch on fire.
My tent might catch on fire, too! Can you tell me
what to do?"
    "Throw some sand on the fire!" says Johnny.
"We'll be there right away!"

How do Pete and Johnny put out the fire?

Why shouldn't children use matches?

What would *you* do if something caught on fire?

The next call for help comes from Mrs. Nelson.

"There is a man with a bulldozer outside my window,"
she says. "He is going to tear down my house to make
room for the new highway!

"But my house has been here for 100 years!
I don't want it torn down. I'm so upset I can't even
drink my tea! Can you help me?"

"Calm yourself, Mrs. Nelson," says Johnny.
"Of course we can help you.
Just go into your garden and drink your tea.
We'll be right there. And we'll bring some ginger beer
for the highway workers."

Pete and Johnny bring lots of ginger beer
for the workers.

Do *you* think they will be able to save
Mrs. Nelson's house?

By the time Pete and Johnny reach Mrs. Nelson's house,
trucks and cranes and tools are everywhere.
The highway workers are digging and hammering.
First, Pete gives ginger beer to all the men.
Then Johnny borrows a giant bulldozer.

He scoops up Mrs. Nelson's house, grass and all,
and carries it far away from the commotion.
"Thank you so much," cries Mrs. Nelson.
"You lost my tea set, but you saved my house!"

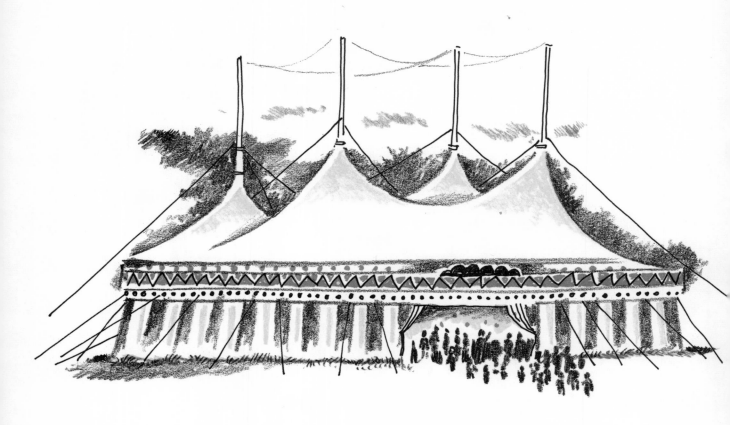

Can you guess who calls for help next?
That's right — the circus master!
  "We're the greatest circus in the whole world," he says.
"But we'll have to cancel our performance today.
Five of our best horses have chicken pox
and they have to stay in bed. The children will be very
disappointed if there is no circus!"

Which horse has the worst case of chicken pox?

Johnny tells the circus master not to cancel the performance.
"We don't have any horses," he says. "But we do have
the smartest, tamest elephant in the whole world!"

Pete is the star of the circus. All the children
love his fancy tricks. He dances on top of a big white ball,
while Johnny balances on his back.

What do *you* like best about the circus?

At three o'clock the telephone is ringing.
When Pete picks up the phone a weak voice says:

"Here we are — five sick old ladies —
in room number 9 at the hospital.
We've been lying here for days and days,
but no one comes to visit us.
We're getting more unhappy every day.
Can you help us?"
"Don't worry," says Johnny.
"We'll be there in no time."

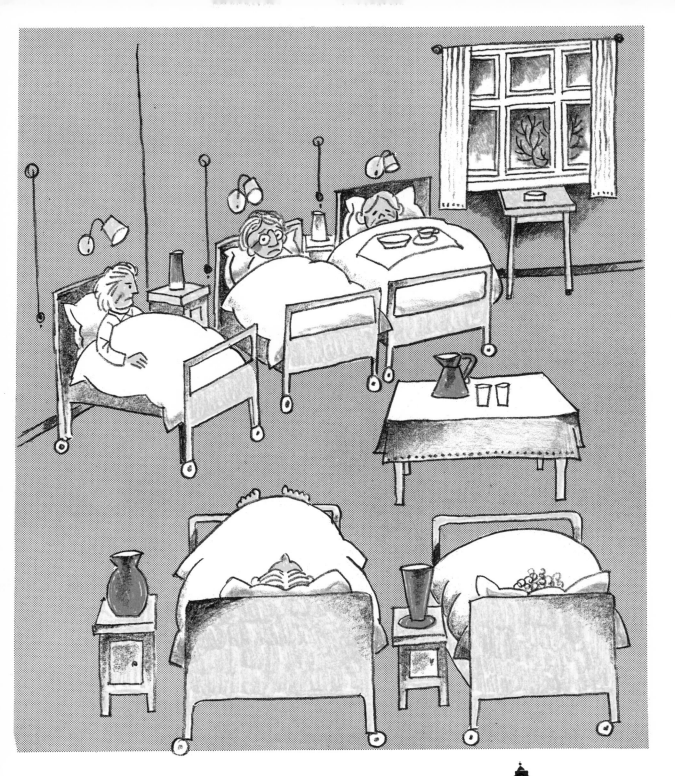

Have *you* ever been sick in the hospital?

What was wrong with you?

Who came to visit you when *you* were sick?

Pete and Johnny bring coffee, cake, and cookies
to the ladies in the hospital.
Pete paints flowers on the walls,
and Johnny puts real flowers
on all the bedside tables.
Soon the room looks bright and cheerful.
   "Thank you," say the five ladies.
"We feel better already
because we are happy."
   "Good-by," say Pete and Johnny
when they have finished their work.
"We hope you get well soon!"

At five o'clock the phone rings once more: *Dingalingaling*!

"Hello, hello," says Johnny. "This is Pete and Johnny's Rescue Squad. We help everyone—"

"You can skip the rest," says the voice. "This is Mrs. Madison at the farm. It's getting late and my husband is not home yet. The radishes have not been watered and the pigs have not been washed. Can you help me?"

"We'll be right there," says Johnny.

Pete and Johnny get to work at once.
First they water the radishes.
How do Pete and Johnny water the radishes?

Then they wash the pigs.
Why do you think pigs have curly tails?

When Pete and Johnny get home the phone is ringing.
"Hello, hello," says Johnny. "This is Pete and Johnny's
Rescue Squad. We help everyone both big and small.
Tell me calmly what has happened and we will come
and help you."

"This is Mrs. Marshall,"
says the voice on the phone.
"Today is my little Albert's birthday.
His friends are here to watch
the children's hour on television.
But the television set is broken.
What shall I do?"

"Calm yourself," says Johnny.
"We will entertain the children."

How do Pete and Johnny
entertain the children?

How many children are watching the show?

At seven o'clock, a call comes from an old woman
who cannot go to the supermarket.
Pete hurries to the market to do the shopping for her.

What is he buying
for the old woman?

"Hello," says Johnny, when the phone rings again.
"Attention!" says a voice at the other end.
"This is Colonel Miller of the town guard.
In exactly one hour we must march through town.
But our drummer is in bed with a sore throat.
Can you help us? Over and out!"
"We'll be there right away,"
says Johnny. "Over and out!"

Can *you* play the drum?

Pete plays the big bass drum for the town guard.
But not many people hear his beautiful music.
Rain and hail begin to fall.

Thunder booms and lightning flashes.
Poor Pete gets soaking wet.
   Did *you* ever get absolutely soaked on a rainy day?

That night Pete comes down with a frightful cold.
He has a runny nose, a cough, and a sore throat.

He has a fever and he doesn't feel like eating or playing games.

He doesn't want ice cream and he won't watch television.

"You are not well," says Johnny. "I'll call the doctor.
He, too, helps everyone — big and small.
He will make you well."

The doctor comes to examine Pete. He thinks
it would be best for Pete to go to the hospital.
What do you think the doctor has in his bag?

Pete goes to the hospital.
The five sick old ladies are in the next room.
Everyone who has been helped by the Rescue Squad
comes to visit Pete. They all want to cheer him up.
And they want to know when he can come home again.

Who comes to visit Pete in the hospital?

Do you remember what Pete and Johnny did
to help each of them?

Do you remember who Miss Lottie is?

A week later Pete feels much better.
His nose doesn't run
and he doesn't have a cough.
He doesn't have a fever
and he feels like eating his food.
He even asks for chewing gum.
He wants to play with Johnny
and watch television
and read picture books.

So Pete is allowed to go home from the hospital.

Shall I read this story again tomorrow night?

ABOUT THE AUTHOR

JØRGEN CLEVIN, a teacher and a citizen of Denmark, was born in 1920. He had his first picture book (*Rasmus*) published in 1945. It was the story of an ostrich and his long journey from Africa to the Copenhagen Zoo. Since that time he has become well known to Danish children through his radio and television programs.

Mr. Clevin has written more than 25 children's books that are popular throughout Europe. *Pete and Johnny to the Rescue,* a sequel to *Pete's First Day at School,* is his second title to be published in the United States.

Library of Congress Cataloging in Publication Data
Clevin, Jørgen.   Pete and Johnny to the rescue.
Johnny and his elephant friend Pete form a rescue squad to return an escaped canary, to cheer up hospital patients, and to otherwise help the people in their town.
Translation of Jakob og Joakims redningskorps.
[1. Neighborliness—Fiction] I. Title.   PZ7.C6214Jak [E] 74-4926   ISBN 0-394-82995-6   ISBN 0-394-92995-0 (lib. bdg.)